VOID

Manvi Arora

BlueRose ONE .com DIY
Stories Matter
NewDelhi • London

BLUEROSE PUBLISHERS
India | U.K.

BlueRose ONE.com DIY
Stories Matter
NewDelhi • London

For permissions requests or inquiries regarding this publication, please contact:

BLUEROSE PUBLISHERS
www.BlueRoseONE.com
info@bluerosepublishers.com
+91 8882 898 898
+4407342408967

ISBN: 978-93-6261-136-9

First Edition: December 2024

To the one without whom each passing day feels like a station missed and a destination left unexplored.

grief: a souvenir of love.

05.10.2019

Prologue

Dreams are like a puzzle hidden inside our minds.

They're a mysterious world, but are they real? That's the puzzling part. In dreams, you never know which door might open or who might step through it. It's like wandering through a maze of endless possibilities. Yet, just as you're exploring this different world, the moment you open your eyes, that world disappears, leaving you back in reality, wondering about the fleeting nature of dreams.

The gate looms before me, wide open. And there he stands, his white kurta pajama swirling in the gentle breeze. I am struck by how young he looks, despite his current age. But as I start to walk towards him, he calls out my name, his voice so strong and sure, and tells me it's time to leave. Instantly, my feet come to a halt and I feel as if the whole house is bearing down on my chest. He turns away from me and as I open my eyes, the weight still remains. For a few moments, I am frozen. I lay there still, trying to process what just happened. And then the realization came crashing down on me like a ton of bricks, leaving me with a thought that nothing would ever be the same again. Life would never be the same again.

14.08.2002

1

Approaching the Station

It was late in the evening and he was packing his stuff since he had to leave for Punjab early in the morning the next day. I sat in the corner, counting the pair of clothes he had packed in order to get an idea of his return. Mumma helped him, and despite his excitement, I was upset since I was not used to staying without him. He was the one who tucked me in at night and told me magical stories and rubbed my head. But with my ongoing exams, I could not accompany him on his trip to Punjab, where most of my paternal family lived.

As the last zipper was closed, my mother placed the bag beside the bed, ready for tomorrow's early departure. That night, he rubbed my head and I requested him for two stories instead of one, knowing it will be a long while until I hear his stories again. He laughed and sent me off to sleep. The next morning, he was already gone by the time I woke up. I searched for any sign of him, hoping he might have missed his train, but he had left.

The clock slowed down as I eagerly waited for him to come back. My mood became noticeably low. Few days later, my result came and I passed with flying colors, but the only thing my teacher enquired was if everything was fine at home since I seemed upset in the class. Mumma explained to her that I was very attached to my grandfather and since he was out of town, I was just missing him a little too much.

Finally, after almost two weeks, he returned. I was overjoyed and eager to greet him at the railway station, practically bouncing with excitement. As he stepped off the train, I ran towards him, wrapping my arms around him. At home, he showed me the gifts he had brought for me, and all of us shared a meal of yellow dal and roti, his favorite dish, that mumma had been making daily since she got married. As the night drew to a close, we fell asleep together, with his stories and magical head massages that made me fall asleep in no time.

That's the kind of bond we shared - inseparable. He was my world, and I spent more time with him than I did with my parents. We didn't need anything or anyone else. Mumma tells me I used to wait with a glass of water in my hand for him to come back from the shop, so I could complain about her to him. He used to shield me from my parents' scolding, like most grandparents do.

Daadi and daddu

Daddu always used to say that he was able to live so many years without a life partner because of me and mumma.

My grandmother passed away when I was just 4 months old, and being a single child, we both found the best company in each other. I spent most of my childhood learning and reading because of daddu. He taught me numerous difficult words, kept me updated on current affairs, and much more. I was like a walking encyclopedia back then; it's funny that I'm not as smart now. But at that time, people would be amazed to see me knowing all that at such a young age. Daddu always emphasized the importance of education, saying it takes you a long way. Back then, I didn't fully grasp it, but looking back now, I realize how everything he taught me at that young age is helping me today. Our routine remained fairly consistent, and we were often together as much as possible. Every morning before I went to school, he would take me to the temple with him. In the temple, he would share stories of different gods, although he always emphasized that there's only one god. He taught me how to grind sandalwood, add some water, and make tilak with it. I used to love doing that. Outside the temple, there were a few ladies who used to sit and beg. There, I would often argue with him to give the beggars 50 rupees instead of just 5. He used to get embarrassed about this and reluctantly ended up giving them 50 rupees. Everyone used to end up being happy.

We would spend our evenings together working on my homework. English was his favorite subject, and he would eagerly read all my literature and grammar books. "Make sentences" became our favorite activity. We would sit for hours crafting sentences with the words I brought home from school, so I could proudly claim that I made them on my own the next day in class, even though it was mostly him. There was a time when he fell seriously ill. Being a naive child, I began to worry that he might not recover, and then who would make sentences with me? This thought haunted me until he eventually recovered and returned to our normal routine.

One day, my bua called him and shared how she made a mistake while filling out a cheque, and how her husband teased her about it. She said it in a light-hearted manner, but daddu took it to heart. The very next day, he urged mumma to learn all about banking tasks so that no one could criticize her, and she could become self-sufficient. He firmly believed in the importance of education and financial literacy, especially for women. Daddu patiently taught mumma how to fill out cheques, make deposits and withdrawals, understand fixed deposits, and handle other banking matters. He even opened a joint bank account in my name, since I was not yet 18. He ensured that I learned everything alongside mumma. By the age of around 10, I could independently manage all banking tasks. Bank staff were often amazed when I visited the bank, but that's how daddu was - imparting invaluable life lessons to our family.

There were times when he used to take me on bicycle rides. I would often convince him to stop at a nearby confectionery store and buy a chocolate or a packet of chips. Whenever he was with me at the shop, I felt carefree because I knew he would never refuse my request. But with time, he could no longer pedal the bicycle, and I started riding the activa. Now it was me who would take him to that same shop to get things. By then, I had matured a little, but I still always bought something because I knew he was with me. He would proudly tell the shopkeeper that I used to bring her here before, and now she brings me here and takes care of me.

Roles had reversed, and so had his health. I grew up, and he grew old. He began falling ill more often. His vision deteriorated, and his hearing weakened. The stops at the confectionery shop on the activa soon got replaced with stops at the chemist shop or our family doctor's house. He would often lie quietly on his bed, lost in his thoughts. He never shared his feelings with anyone. He kept his pains and problems to himself, always smiling and saying everything was fine when asked. I suppose my father and I learned not to share our feelings from him. Soon, we all got accustomed to keeping our feelings to ourselves. What was once a family of four, gradually became just four people residing under the same roof.

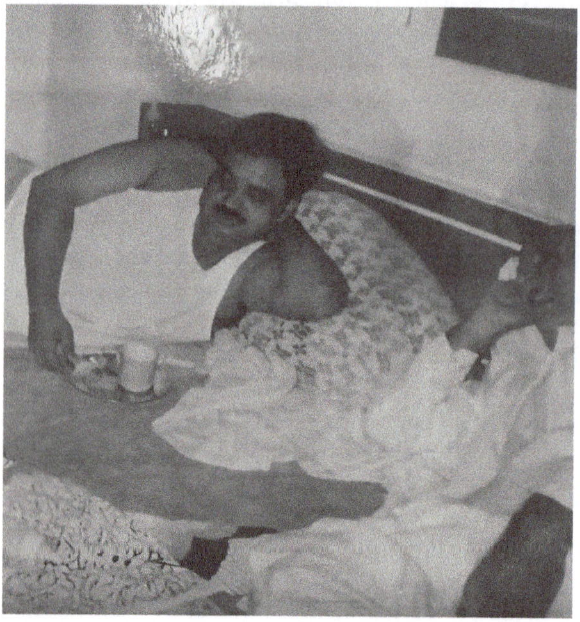

Papa and daddu looking at me

Genes! It's amazing to see both of them laying in the same pose and looking at me.

As time passed, the bond we shared began to fray at the edges. It was as if a void had formed between us, and no matter how hard we tried to bridge the gap, it only seemed to widen. They say an old aged person becomes a child after a certain time and I guess I was not ready to accept him like that. Our conversations were often forced and awkward, our views always clashing. It was as if we were speaking different languages and living in different worlds. I struggled to understand what had brought us to this point. Was it the passing of time, the distance between us, or simply the inescapable weight of our differences? I couldn't say for sure. But despite our growing apart, I could never bring myself to lose the love and respect that I held for him.

There were moments when we still found solace in each other's company, when the shadows of our disagreements lifted and we were able to simply be together. I would sit by his side, listening to him as he spoke of his life and the world that he had known. And in those moments, I would be transported back to a time when we were just inseparable, before the world had begun to pull us apart. It wasn't easy, this new reality that we found ourselves in. But perhaps it was just the natural order of things - the cycle of life, of growth and change and the shifting tides of our relationships. Though the bond that we shared may have been frayed, it was still there, a thread that bound us together through the twists and turns of life. But probably that is how the seasons of life and relations change, with the course of time. Things indeed changed with time, but the concern never faded. I remained the only person in the house who could persuade him to take his medicines without him becoming agitated, while he remained the only one who would let me buy an extra chocolate without scolding me.

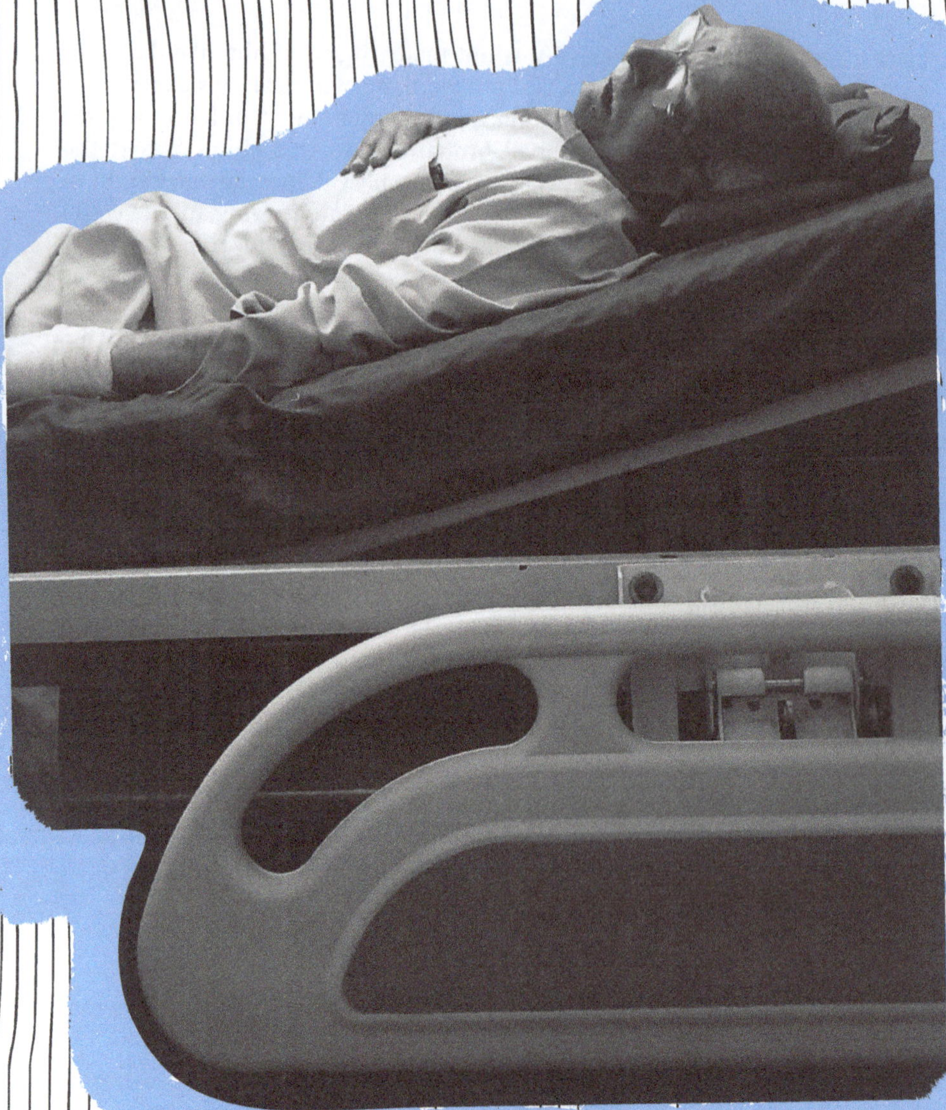

24.11.2021

2

Platform Change

Life changes every day, and ours was no different. Some changes are desired, while others are beyond our control. The latter are the most frightening, as they seem to rest in the hands of a higher power. What's destined to happen will occur, regardless of our attachments. We cherished our home, house number 510, sector 7, despite its numerous issues. It was where my parents got married, where I was born and I grew up, and where countless memories were made. However, every good thing has an expiration date. The condition of the house was deteriorating, with new problems cropping up regularly. With just two rooms, I needed a separate space. Repairing it wasn't an option; it needed to be demolished and rebuilt, which meant a significant investment. Papa was reluctant to spend so much money and favored selling the house to buy or build a new one. We'd been discussing this for years and had listed the house for sale long ago. Many people visited but none made an offer; perhaps it wasn't the right time. One evening, a family visited and, unexpectedly, returned with an offer. Daddu, Mumma, and I weren't keen on selling; we had grown attached to the house and loved the neighborhood. However, Papa had his own reasons and wanting a home closer to the shop for convenience topped them all.. Despite our reservations, fate had its way. On May 18, 2021, I was making lasagna since Shweta, my best friend, was about to leave for Canada very soon and she had been wanting to eat it. I had gone along with papa to surprise her with lasagna. On our way back home, papa received a call from the property dealer informing us that the prospective buyers were ready to make an offer. It was surreal to think that while I indulged in lasagna, the home where I was born and raised was being sold. Everything happened swiftly, leaving us little time to process. Daddu never voiced his feelings, but he had built that house and spent almost 35 years of his life there. Yet, his unconditional love for Papa kept him silent.

In the next six months, we purchased a new house and prepared to move in. However, just a day before the scheduled move, on November 20, 2021, daddu fell severely ill. He had developed a UTI, and his body was shivering uncontrollably. While we were busy with packing and shifting preparations, daddu's health deteriorated rapidly. Papa rushed home with medicines and fruits to help stabilize him. By the next morning, November 21, the moving day, daddu seemed to have improved slightly, so Papa took him to the new house early in the morning. Meanwhile, Mumma and I stayed behind to oversee the shifting process. Little did we know, daddu's condition worsened again while we were busy with the move. Papa urgently called both my buas to come over as he was deeply concerned about daddu's health. While Papa went to fetch them, daddu's condition took a turn for the worse within those few minutes. When Papa returned, he found daddu shivering again. He then took him to the hospital and got all the required tests done. At around 8 PM, we had just bid our final farewell to the old house and arrived at the new one. That's when we learned about daddu's deteriorating health. Stepping into the new house, I was greeted by the sight of cardboard boxes scattered everywhere, and daddu lay in my parents' bedroom. I approached him, giving him a gentle hug and whispering that I had returned. At that moment, my eyes welled up with tears. I hugged him again before rushing to the washroom to compose myself. It's hard to say what triggered those tears – the excitement of moving into a new house, the sadness of leaving the old one behind, daddu's illness, or perhaps a combination of all these emotions.

The following days were incredibly challenging. We were in the midst of shifting to our new home, daddu's health was deteriorating, and then unexpectedly, my nani fell off her balcony, leaving her bedridden. It was an overwhelming situation to handle all at once. His recurring UTIs became a common occurrence for us. Every few weeks, he would fall ill again, drained from within. Fever, loss of appetite, and exhaustion plagued him, leaving him bedridden and sleeping throughout the day. Despite starting antibiotics, they eventually proved ineffective. When he fell ill again, we anticipated it and promptly had his tests done. Our fears were confirmed: the infection had returned, worse than before. The doctor prescribed medication and had to resort to using a urine bag since he lacked the strength to visit the washroom. Although uncomfortable, it was the only practical solution. Seeing him so weak and lifeless, refusing to eat, weighed heavily on everyone, especially papa, who often broke down at daddu's condition. Daddu didn't like hospitals at all (nobody does), but his deteriorating health left no choice. Papa decided to admit him. He was barely conscious of the situation due to his weakness. We called an ambulance to transport him to the hospital. Tears welled in my eyes as they placed him on the stretcher and into the ambulance. Mumma reassured him, urging him to recover and return home soon, but he was not in his senses to reply back to her. I wiped away my tears, accompanying papa to the hospital. Daddu spent a day in the emergency ward before being transferred to the ICU. While the reports were discouraging, the doctors remained optimistic about his recovery.

The next day, as the clock striked 11, I entered a large room filled with rows of beds, each separated by sky blue curtains. The space was crowded and suffocating, with the constant sound of footsteps racing about. I scanned the room, searching for one bed in particular, bed number 510, which also happened to be our old house number. Eventually, I spotted it and approached it, only to find him lying there with tubes and pipes attached to his weak and feeble body. Tears streamed down my face as I tried to put on a brave smile and greet him. His eyes met mine, and a faint smile spread across his mouth, as if he had been waiting for me. A huge pipe was there inside his mouth that was the only source of feeding him then. Though he could no longer speak much, he raised his hand to indicate that he was doing fine. Struggling to speak, he managed to whisper, "I am perfectly alright." My eyes filled with tears at his words. A doctor approached me and asked me to come closer to the table next to my daddu's bed. I could see the distress on his face, and my heart sank. As he opened his register, he delivered the news that I had been afraid of. Each word he spoke, confirmed the worst. Despite our attempts to avoid the inevitable, my daddu's condition was deteriorating rapidly and his organs were failing one by one. The tears that had already welled up in my eyes began to flow freely. I felt a sense of numbness took over me, but when I looked back at my daddu, I could see that he was concerned about my well-being. He raised his finger and motioned for me to stop crying. Trying to say something, he mumbled unclear words that I struggled to understand. After several attempts, he gave up and placed his hand on my shoulder as a sign of his blessings. I looked at him one last time, and he directed my gaze towards the clock, which read 11:50 am. I understood he wanted me to leave before the visiting hours were over but I also sensed he was trying to hide his emotions in front of me. I held his hand tightly with a thought if I would be able to do that again. I told him that I would be back soon and began to leave, passing by another old patient on my way out. Watching two young kids play in the corridor, I watched as their mother convinced the security guard to let them meet their grandfather, who was also in the ICU, since children are not allowed inside the ICU room. The old patient, I saw earlier, joined them at the door, and the kids had a heartwarming conversation about him coming back home soon. As I stood there, looking at them, I realized how different yet similar our situations were. I longed to have my daddu come home and talk to me again, to relive all those moments with him, but I knew it was impossible. All I could do then was to pray that his suffering ended soon.

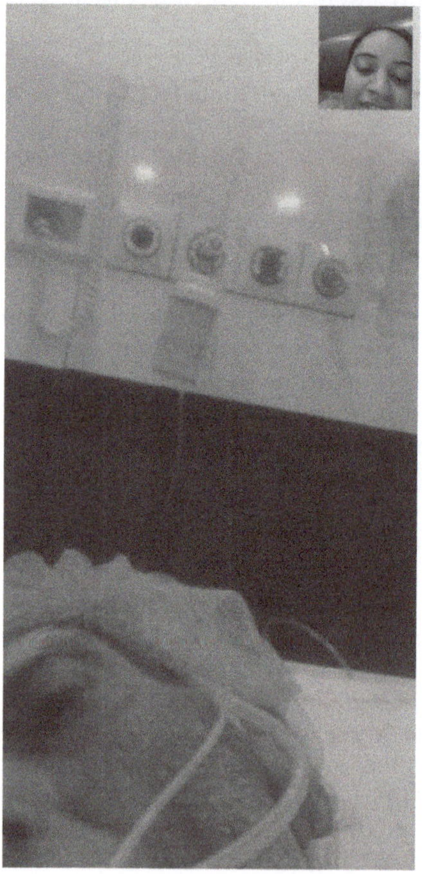

Our first and last video call

I video called mumma to have a look at daddu, while she was at the hospital. I tried my best to control my tears but could not. Nothing felt in control.

On our way back home, Papa and I experienced a mixture of bittersweet emotions. We were undoubtedly saddened by my daddu's deteriorating condition, yet there was a glimmer of happiness within us. Today, he had made an effort to communicate, and that gave us a sliver of hope. That's the thing about the ICU - you're torn between staying by your loved one's side and the necessity of abiding by hospital regulations. It's a constant battle of emotions. During the evening visiting hours, I decided to stay home while Mumma accompanied Papa to see daddu. Through a video call, I caught a brief glimpse of him. He could hear my voice, but faintly, as mumma conveyed my words to him. However, this time, he remained silent. When mumma and papa returned home, their expressions told a very depressing tale. His condition had worsened, and he could no longer utter a single word. He made futile attempts to communicate, desperately trying to express something that was beyond their understanding. They even offered him a pen, hoping he could write it down, but his body refused to cooperate. Probably, he was trying to say the same thing which he wanted to tell me in the morning. I still yearn to decode the meaning behind his silent efforts. Perhaps, someday, in his own unique way, he will reveal his message to me. Days blended together as we anxiously awaited the designated visiting hours. Each passing moment carried an underlying fear, knowing that any news could arrive at any time. Whenever our phones rang, our hearts skipped a beat as we scanned the caller ID, hoping it would be an update from the hospital. Nights proved to be the most daunting. Sleep eluded us as our minds wandered, consumed by thoughts of him and the uncertain future. Appetites diminished, and the act of eating became an afterthought, overshadowed by the weight of our worries. Sleep took a backseat as we remained on high alert, attentive and prepared for any development that could unfold.

Those days when he was in the hospital were really tough for us. We all felt so powerless. But it was papa who seemed to feel it the most. It was strange to see him so emotional—I'd never seen that side of him before. He'd break down often, and whenever I saw him upset, tears would start flowing from my eyes too. I remember one of those days when Papa was already at the hospital. I had just showered and was getting ready to go there too. Both my buas were also planning to come that day. Mom suggested that maybe I shouldn't go since so many people were already there. I simply replied, "If I don't go now, then when will I?" No more words were exchanged. I guess, deep down, we both knew what the days ahead held for us.

A few years ago, I found out I had kidney stones, and boy, did they hurt! For a long while, I toughed it out, trying all sorts of medicines and home remedies.

Then, one day, the pain became unbearable, and a check-up revealed the ugly truth: I had a massive 17mm stone in my left kidney and a 12mm one in my right. With such large stones, there was no room for debate—I needed surgery. Papa, always worried about my health, quickly decided to go ahead with the surgery. We talked to many doctors, sifting through all their advice, until we settled on a plan. The doctor, after careful inspection, recommended a plan. We'd go ahead with surgery on my left kidney and start medications to break down the 12mm stone in my right kidney. Lots of tests, paperwork, and preparations later, we had a date set for my operation. But there was one person we kept in the dark—my dear daddu. He was a sensitive soul, and we didn't want to worry him. Our plan meant we'd be away from home for three days. My masi stepped in to stay at home and take care of daddu while we were gone. But daddu, sharp as a tack, sensed something was off. He felt the change in our routine and started asking questions. He wondered where my mom was and if everything was alright between my parents. Then, he turned his attention to me, and his questions got more urgent. My masi tried to give vague answers, trying to keep things normal. But daddu's worry just grew, and after hours of stress, he asked the same questions again. My masi couldn't keep it from him any longer, so she told him everything. She reassured him that I was safe, just having surgery and I'll be home very soon. When I got out of the hospital and came back home, I went straight to daddu's room. He saw me, with a smile on his face, and started asking me questions. I answered every one of them, trying to ease his fears. Then, we locked eyes, and I saw a tear in his eye. He told me he couldn't stand to see me in pain and had been so worried. I comforted him, telling him not to worry. Two different situations, but both filled with the same anticipation, fear, and even the same hospital. The only difference was the outcome—I came back to him healthy.

It had been 2-3 days since he was admitted to the hospital. It was a Sunday evening, around 8 pm. We were at home, and he was still in the hospital. One of Papa's friends had come over, and Mumma and I were in our respective rooms. Mumma was on the phone with a relative when I heard Papa calling my name urgently, asking me to accompany him to the hospital. He mentioned that he'd received a call from the hospital informing him that daddu had been put on a ventilator. It felt like the world had come crashing down. I was at a loss for words, bewildered by the news. Quickly informing Mumma, I left home with Papa and his friend, heading to the hospital, which was barely 5-7 minutes away. On that journey, all I could do was pray with all my heart. The uncertainty left me feeling like we might have already lost him, as the lack of clear information and our earlier apprehensions made it seem inevitable.

When everything seems to vanish, it's God we turn to. He becomes a magician, a beacon of hope, and a comforter. His name flows from our lips as if by instinct. In every hospital, there's a place of worship because when science reaches its limits, prayers step in. As we walked into the hospital, I caught sight of the temple and instinctively joined my hands, bowing my head in front of the almighty, seeking solace and protection for daddu. We hurried straight to the second floor where the ICU ward was located. Upon reaching the main door, we found it locked as it wasn't visiting hours. Trying another route, a security guard intercepted us, being rude and questioning our presence. We explained we received a call from the hospital, stressing the urgency, but he refused entry. Papa, already stressed, became furious. Thankfully, an old nurse intervened, calming the situation and instructing me to obtain a visitor's pass from the reception. Rushing downstairs, I quickly got the pass made, then sprinted back upstairs. Papa had already gone inside, and his friend urged me to join. Unfamiliar with the ward's location, we stumbled upon Sunny bhaiya, our old neighbor's nephew. He guided us to the correct ward, where daddu lay on the ventilator, surrounded by tubes and his eyes shut. Sunny bhaiya examined his reports, revealing multiple organ failures leading to the ventilator support. We were called to sign some documents. While Papa handled the formalities courageously, I was overwhelmed, devastated by the sight of him lying there. Tears streamed down my face as I watched him motionless. I could see him leaving us all. I can't recall much after that until we returned home.

Upon returning home, we shared the distressing news with our close relatives. The heaviness of the situation was felt all around us. After the flurry of phone calls, silence surrounded us, interrupted only by occasional moments of emotional breakdowns. In the quiet of that moment, the three of us were lost in our own thoughts. I often wonder what Mumma and Papa might have been pondering, but for me, it was a deep fear, a feeling of facing something unavoidable. Memories flooded my mind, reflecting my deep-seated fear of losing loved ones. That night, I can't recall if any of us ate, or even when we finally drifted off to sleep. The intensity of emotions took over, leaving us in a state of emotional turmoil.

17.02.2022

3

Arrival

Waking to a day weighed down by unspoken sorrow, each breath carries the quiet anticipation of an approaching emotional storm. The next day was anticipated to be an emotional roller coaster, and indeed it was. It was like the nervous anticipation on a result day when the odds are against you, and you cling to hope for a miracle. Papa had already left for the hospital before I woke up. It felt like a decisive day, one where things would change. Both my buas were on their way to the hospital. Upon reaching, I saw Papa sitting outside the ICU ward, visibly shattered with teary eyes. He quickly wiped his tears upon seeing me. Outside the closed ICU door, with its circular glass windows, I anxiously waited for visiting hours to begin. Peeping through, I caught a glimpse of Daddu, his bed now in the center of the ward. Lifeless, he lay there. Soon both my buas arrived. When the clock struck 11, marking the beginning of visiting hours, we hurried inside. I entered first with Papa, and it was a flood of tears. I couldn't hold back my tears. Papa had a discussion with the doctor, and in the meantime, one of my buas and her son joined us. Emotions overwhelmed everyone, and witnessing their tears made me cry even more. Before leaving, I firmly held his lifeless hand and silently apologized to him in my heart for any unintentional hurt I might have caused. I'm not sure why I did it, but it felt necessary. It felt like the heartfelt moment of saying goodbye at a railway station or airport, where you keep looking back, waving, trying to hold onto the presence of your loved ones for as long as possible. We all came out and sat in silence. No one uttered a word for the first few minutes. Later, we went down to the waiting area, and from the conversations among the elders, it was evident that a decision needed to be made—the decision to remove the ventilator and bring him back home. Papa and my uncle sent all of us home. I was lost in my thoughts, with memories, his voice, my fears, and much more swirling in my head. We all returned home and shared the updates with Mumma, who was waiting alone. A couple of hours later, Bua called uncle for an update. He mentioned they had requested discharge, and the formalities were in progress. They were bringing Daddu home that day itself.

The weather turned cloudy, and Papa had asked me to return some of Daddu's unused medicines to the chemist. Around 5 in the evening, I went to the chemist to return the medicines. As soon as I stepped outside the medical shop, it started raining heavily. I waited under a shelter, lost in my countless thoughts. After about 20 minutes, the rain stopped, and I thought of leaving. I went from the road that took a turn for home near the hospital itself. There was a railway crossing, closed due to an approaching train. As I waited for it to open, my eyes fell on an ambulance ahead in the traffic. A vague thought crossed my mind that Daddu might be in this ambulance. As soon as the train passed, I raced my Activa and soon caught up, moving just behind it. I could see Papa and uncle in the car leading the ambulance. I felt numb because in my head bringing Daddu home meant bringing his lifeless body. I had thought that as soon as the doctors would remove the ventilator, he would leave us. When we all reached home, Mumma and buas were waiting outside. The ambulance door opened, and I saw ward boys bringing Daddu, with a large oxygen cylinder. Observing, I understood. He was still alive, still breathing. The hospital didn't provide the oxygen pump, so Papa arranged for a manual one. Someone had to manually pump oxygen for him. Seeing the ambulance, a few neighbors came.

The whole evening passed in making necessary arrangements. Meanwhile, Daddu's nephews arrived. Daddu was very attached to them, and vice versa. They respected him greatly and were grateful for all he had done for them. Everyone took turns pumping oxygen for him. The house quickly filled up with relatives from all around. Everyone took turns pumping oxygen, with the elders handling it during the day and my cousin and I taking over at night. We alternated pumping, one after the other, until around 4 in the morning or until someone else woke up to take over.

We were pumping oxygen, but apart from that, his body seemed frozen, his eyes fixed on the wall, surrounded by numerous tubes. There was a strange sense of relief that he was still with us, alive, but was he truly living? Did he deserve to endure so much suffering? These thoughts raced through my mind, and likely through the minds of others who witnessed his suffering. The more people gathered, the more suggestions poured in. Everyone had their own idea of what should be done, each opinion adding to the cacophony of voices filling the room. During that period, there were multiple occasions when we believed it was his time to depart. He'd start breathing heavily or show some other sign, leading everyone to gather around his bed in tears. However, he would soon return to normal, and we would resume our activities. It felt like we nearly missed the train but managed to catch it just in time.

In Indian culture, myths and superstitions often play a significant role. Observing his intense suffering, some relatives started suggesting their own set of chants and traditional remedies, hoping for him to depart peacefully. My mother even recited passages from the Bhagavad Gita, believed to assist the soul in departing peacefully. Since he was deeply attached to me, a few relatives suggested that I whisper in his ear, urging him to let go, assuring him that we would be okay without him. But actually doing it was far more difficult than merely suggesting it. While their intentions were undoubtedly kind, the urge to hold on was strong, and no matter what, I couldn't bring myself to let him go. There was a sense that as long as he was with us, everything remained stable, but the moment he would leave, the impending storm would shatter our world. The environment was similar to the anticipation one feels while waiting for a train before relocating to a new city and there is a strange ache in the chest before leaving everything behind.

In a sense, pain has a way of bringing people closer together, and those few days brought our family closer than ever. We could clearly see the legacy of love and respect that daddu had built throughout his life. He was a generous soul. He helped everyone to the best of his ability. Anyone who had ever encountered him had nothing but wonderful things to say. As a family, we witnessed this reality unfolding before our eyes. Life has a way of coming full circle. The nephews whom he had once supported and helped to stand on their feet during their times of need were now by his side, in his final days, pumping oxygen for him. Another touching aspect of those days was the enduring bond between him, me, and papa. Despite his eyes being fixed on the ceiling, whenever either of us broke down in front of him, tears would well up in his eyes or they would turn red. There were even moments when take hold. You're rooted in place, uncertain of the train's arrival time. We found ourselves in a similar state, waiting for something that would devastate us, but there was no going back. It was evident that some people in the room were in a rush. Logically, they might have been right, but our emotions were controlling our actions. We simply weren't prepared to let go. There comes a moment when overwhelming emotions themselves become sources of distress. I suppose we had reached that point. We knew a man named Wilson who worked at a hospital. He had visited our house before when daddu was unwell, bathing him and administering his injections. This time too, we called him to change daddu's drip. It had been two days since daddu returned home. On the third morning, when Wilson came to change the drip, he advised Papa that we should stop pumping oxygen as it was only prolonging daddu's suffering. Reluctantly, Papa agreed, and we stopped the pumping. By the time I woke up, all this had already happened. When I entered the room and noticed that nobody was pumping oxygen, I immediately questioned Papa. The pain and confusion were quite evident on his face. Papa, whom I had always seen as a practical man, had been overwhelmed by emotions during those days. It was a rare sight to see him break down, behaving like a lost child in a fair, looking for his father.

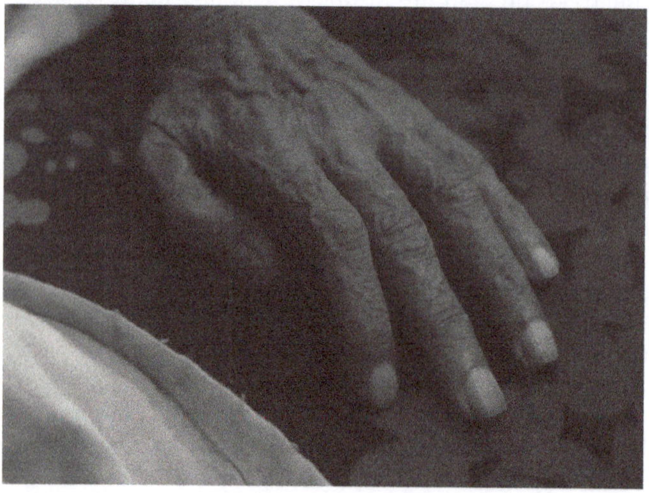

His last few days with us

Who knew those were the last few days he had with us we had with him. Does anyone ever know?

During those days, whenever I was with daddu, whether simply sitting by his side or pumping oxygen, I couldn't help but stare at him intently. I would talk to him, feeling remorseful for all the moments I hadn't spent with him.

The song *Lag Ja Gale* would play in my head continuously, its lyrics and emotions resonating so deeply that tears would automatically well up in my eyes. I feel very conscious when revealing my emotions in front of others. It seems to me that displaying my vulnerable side makes me appear weak. So, when I was alone with daddu, I would hold his hand and recall all the good memories we shared together. I can still vividly recall the sensation of his touch. The lines on his hand had softened with age, leaving behind smooth, cold skin. I clung to that old and fragile hand for as long as I could.

The day passed quickly, almost unnoticed. There came a moment when we felt we lost him, but that soon dissipated. It was lunch time and since there were a lot of people in the house, we had hired a lady to cook food since mumma had to look after other things as well. That day, I took charge of serving, insisting that my mother eat first while I served others. Once the meal was done, everyone dispersed - some for a stroll, others attending to their needs. I sat on the dining table to have my meal. Papa felt a drop in his sugar levels, so my bua gave him a plump to eat. It was just those few minutes when daddu was alone in the room. Then, a sudden call rang through the house, breaking the calm. Everyone rushed inside. Daddu's breathing became heavy, and panic gripped us all. I sat down on the floor near his face with mumma on my side who had held his hand. Tears streamed down our faces. I frantically started pumping oxygen, hoping to save him, but my uncle's voice broke through, urging me to accept the inevitable, to let him go peacefully. I watched helplessly as my parents crumbled before my eyes. Within just a few minutes, at around 3:30 pm, the train of life pulled away from the platform and we were left stranded alone on the platform, in a sea of sorrow and grief. No matter how hard we tried, we couldn't catch that train.

11.06.2022

4

Post Departure

There is often a moment of silence as a train departs from the station, and soon the hustle resumes as if nothing happened. I don't remember what happened after that. Everyone got busy calling and informing others about the demise. It's weird how we start addressing the person in past tense. It's weird how we start referring to the person as merely a body and not a human. Soon the house was filled with so many people who came to offer their condolences. I saw people whom I hadn't seen in many years. Moments after the loss of a loved one feel surreal, like a dream, but everyone keeps expressing their sorrow, which serves as a reminder that it is not. Max had always been a hyperactive dog. We kept him in my parents' room, and to everyone's surprise, he slept there quietly, as if he understood what had happened. Papa's friends took care of all the tent and food arrangements, so we didn't have to worry about anything. We didn't feel like eating, but our relatives insisted that we eat some food.

We had placed daddu or if I may say, daddu's body in a refrigerator as the cremation was scheduled for the next day. That night, all of his nephews, my buas, my parents, and I gathered around him. Each person started sharing stories of their memories with him, recounting what he had done for them and describing the kind of person he was. It was such an emotional atmosphere listening to everyone. As we shared those stories, everyone gradually drifted off to sleep. That night, I thought about him a lot before falling asleep with his memories still on my mind. The next day when I woke up, my tears flowed like a river, unstoppable. I tried to get hold of myself, but my body won't obey. Desperately, I searched for my mother, and I could hear the sounds of people moving and murmuring throughout the house. Through the translucent glass door, I spotted her sitting on the sofa, and without hesitation, I opened it and rushed next to her. I was still crying as I poured out my dream, where daddu told me that it was time to leave. She pulled me close, trying to comfort me for something even she knew could not be undone. I spotted my masi, who must have reached early morning from Noida, sitting next to my mother. As I looked around the room, I saw the faces of a few other relatives, some crying silently, others lost in their own thoughts. And there, in the middle of it all, lay my daddu, still and silent, his body covered in a white dupatta that billowed with each passing breath of air from the fan, giving me a hope of him breathing. But it was just a false hope and my mind was playing tricks with me. Deep down, no matter how much I tried to not accept this fact, even I knew that he was gone, forever.

His beloved room

The room has everything but you. It's empty.

The first day of grief is incredibly surreal. They're not here anymore, but it's like they just left. They're gone, but it doesn't quite sink in. You can't be with them, yet you were just with them. You know they're not coming back, but there's a lingering feeling that they might. Coping with death is tough because your mind is used to feeling emotions for someone, and even after they're gone, it still expects to feel those emotions for them, almost like a reflex.

And sometimes, we resist healing because the pain is the final connection to what we've lost, and grief is essentially love that has nowhere to go. Life after losing a loved one to death is often marked by loneliness, a loneliness that many people may not fully understand. Over time, this loneliness becomes a sort of new normal, but every now and then, waves of grief wash over you, reminding you that this loneliness was never normal and that it's absurd to believe otherwise. However, grieving is a natural process, and it often surfaces unexpectedly. It's like when you have blisters in your mouth, and your tongue accidentally touches them, causing a sudden, strange pain. Grief is that pain. Just like those blisters, you need to acknowledge grief. You need to sit with it and allow yourself to feel it fully.

Whenever someone asked me about my greatest fear, I used to say it was the fear of losing my loved ones. I hadn't experienced death in my family so closely before. This was the first time something like this happened right in front of my eyes. I witnessed his soul departing from his body right before me, and I didn't know how to cope with it. I didn't know who to talk to because everyone around me was also grieving, and I didn't want to burden them further. That's when loneliness crept in. My close friend Shweta, with whom I could share anything, was miles away. Though I had a few friends in college, I hadn't known them for very long. Dealing with everything alone was very difficult but now it's been almost two years since daddu passed away. Not a day goes by when I don't think about him or remember something he said or did. I suppose I'll have to hold onto his memory for longer than I knew him.

As I gaze at the stars, I can't help but wonder if he is watching over me. Does he see me pouring my thoughts onto paper or losing myself in books for hours and smile back at me? I often think about how proud he would have been of me, if he was around, when I wrote my own book, a dedication to him. But at the same time, I can't help but feel the weight of his absence and how much I miss him everyday. As I look at his old bed, the only piece of old furniture we still have in the new house, I am reminded of our shared room and the memories we created together. It still has "Manvi's and daddu's room" written on its back. His walking stick brings back the sound of it banging on the floor, a reminder of his determination to walk on his own, even when his body no longer cooperated. The blood pressure monitor takes me back to those early mornings when he would wake me up to check his blood pressure, which he used to always guess before I told him the exact readings. And as I glance at the photo frame on the wall with flowers draped around it, it feels as though he is showering me with his blessings from beyond. His physical presence may have left the house, but his absence has left an unfillable void.

It's touching how the sight of elderly people on the bus now reminds me of him. I wish I could hold his hands again, feel their warmth and reassurance. The memory of his hands lingers in my thoughts- the loose skin, the nearly faded lines on the palms. Now, all they can do is send blessings from above, watching me over from a place of peace. Love transcends time and space, and I know his spirit is always with me. It's natural to feel a sense of guilt when the spaces between missing someone grow longer. The pain of remembering a loved one can indeed feel like a stab to the heart, reminding us of the depth of our emotions. Cherishing the memories and allowing yourself to miss them whenever you feel the need is a way to keep the connection alive, even across the boundaries of time. Grief doesn't have a timeline; it comes and goes in waves, and it's okay to embrace those moments of missing with both sorrow and love. It might take a little longer to accept it, but I will, hopefully soon. Nonetheless, I hope he realizes that I never stopped loving him and surely, never will.

Manvi's room and dadu's room

The house has all the new furniture except this bed. It is a reminder that no matter what, it will always be Manvi and daddu's room.

Sometimes, everything seems normal, just an ordinary day, and then out of nowhere, you stumble upon something unexpected. It could be a piece of paper tucked in an old journal, and suddenly, it's like getting hit with a wave of memories. That's the tricky thing about emotions and memories—they're a bit like the weather, completely unpredictable. You might be feeling okay one moment, and the next, something small triggers a flood of memories and flashbacks of someone who's no longer here with you. It's surprising and overwhelming, catching you off guard when you least expect it. Aadi, daddu's nephew's son, who I think had a different connection with him altogether. The innocence of a child's questions and the memories associated with him bring both warmth and pain. It is very difficult to explain his absence, especially to a little one who still wants to talk to his "Ambala daadu." When someone asks about a loved one who's not here anymore, it's like a surprise punch to the heart. It's a mix of feelings—a big sad feeling, a wish they were still here, and remembering the good times. There have been several instances where people have asked me about him or his health and I get numb and helpless and I have to tell them that he is no more. Goodbyes are rarely easy. But I suppose that these feelings of being helpless and numb are completely natural and hopefully will disappear soon.

Endings are destined, but they never come with warnings, and ultimately, everyone passes away, especially those left behind. Missing someone after they die is like waves breaking on the shore, each one carrying a piece of your heart away. Life goes on, with or without them, but grief, it always stays. I might have written all these words with a hope that I would end up with no more grieving. But no matter how many books are written or words are said about grief, the human world never runs out of it. Each passing moment feels like a betrayal, yet, amidst the pain, there's a strange comfort in knowing that their presence still lingers. I will continue to miss him every day, with a subconscious feeling that he is somewhere around. I will talk to him in my head whenever I have questions or feel lonely. I will always keep his photograph with me and give him the first bite of the cake on my birthday. I will always gaze at the sky, knowing he is watching over me from the world above. I will keep going on in life, for him, though, his absence will always remain like a constant ache in my heart, a void that can never be filled. His presence might not be, but his memory will be my guiding light through the darkest of days ahead.

I'll always long to hop on that train, but maybe it just rolled away, taking with it our shared laughter and your love, leaving me stranded in a station of memories.

14.08.2023

Epilogue

It's been over two years since you appeared in my dreams, softly whispering that it was time to depart. Yet, you haven't truly left me. Your presence lingers, visiting me in my dreams, always in our old house, indulging in Marie biscuits. While we don't prepare dal every day anymore, when we do, I raise my plate just a bit, as if to share the news with you. Papa still remains stubborn, unwilling to heed my advice, and there's no one to scold him, not even you. So, maybe if you could, a little. Will you still take his side, like you always did? Birthdays, never a big deal for me, now feel heavier, burdened with your absence. But I promise to carry your photo along with me and give you the first bite of the cake. The flowers you lovingly planted have withered away, perhaps needed more in your heavenly garden. The clock in your room often stops, as if trying to narrate its own tale. I've immersed myself in reading, meticulously correcting others' grammar and spelling errors—a testament to your teachings. Aren't you proud? Papa and mumma ache for you deeply, though no one misses you as much as I do.

Life, it seems, will never be the same again.

See, I made all these sentences alone.

Acknowledgements

Writing this book has been a journey of trying to navigate grief and loss, but along the way, I've discovered that it's much more than just that. My hope is that these pages will reach anyone who is mourning or struggling to break free from the painful cycle of losing a loved one—especially a grandparent.

It feels quite ironic to acknowledge my Daddu—to whom this book is dedicated—because he was the one who first introduced me to the world of reading and writing. Without his love for stories and words, I might not have found the courage to put my thoughts on paper. Thank you, Daddu, for all the subtle signs along the way and for gently nudging me towards completing this book.

This journey wouldn't have been possible without the unwavering guidance and vision of Ms. Deeksha Kumar. Your insights and encouragement shaped this book into what it is today. Thank you for your invaluable support.

Lastly, to my family and friends—thank you for your endless love, patience, and encouragement throughout this emotional journey. Your presence gave me the strength to finish what I started.

This book is as much a part of me as it is a tribute to him. I hope it helps others heal, just as writing it has helped me.